Teachers, librarians, and kids from across Canada are talking about the *Canadian Flyer Adventures*. Here's what some of them had to say:

Great Canadian historical content, excellent illustrations, and superb closing historical facts (I love the kids' commentary!). ~ *SARA S., TEACHER, ONTARIO*

As a teacher–librarian I welcome this series with open arms. It fills the gap for Canadian historical adventures at an early reading level! There's fast action, interesting, believable characters, and great historical information. ~ *MARGARET L., TEACHER–LIBRARIAN, BRITISH COLUMBIA*

The *Canadian Flyer Adventures* will transport young readers to different eras of our past with their appealing topics. Thank goodness there are more artifacts in that old dresser ... they are sure to lead to even more escapades. ~ *SALLY B., TEACHER–LIBRARIAN, MANITOBA*

When I shared the book with a grade 1–2 teacher at my school, she enjoyed the book, noting that her students would find it appealing because of the action-adventure and short chapters. ~ *HEATHER J., TEACHER AND LIBRARIAN, NOVA SCOTIA*

Newly independent readers will fly through each *Canadian Flyer Adventure*, and be asking for the next installment! Children will enjoy the fast-paced narrative, the personalities of the main characters, and the drama of the dangerous situations the children find themselves in. ~ *PAM L., LIBRARIAN, ONTARIO*

I love the fact that these are Canadian adventures—kids should know how exciting Canadian history is. Emily and Matt are regular kids, full of curiosity, and I can see readers relating to them. ~ *JEAN K., TEACHER, ONTARIO*

What kids told us:

I would like to have the chance to ride on a magical sled and have adventures. ~ *EMMANUEL*

I would like to tell the author that her book is amazing, incredible, awesome, and a million times better than any book I've read. ~ *MARIA*

I would recommend the *Canadian Flyer Adventures* series to other kids so they could learn about Canada too. The book is just the right length and hard to put down. ~ *PAUL*

The books I usually read are the full-of-fact encyclopedias. This book is full of interesting ideas that simply grab me. ~ *ELEANOR*

At the end of the book Matt and Emily say they are going on another adventure. I'm very interested in where they are going next! ~ *ALEX*

I like when Emily and Matt fly into the sky on a sled towards a new adventure. I can't wait for the next book! ~ *JI SANG*

Hurry, Freedom

Frieda Wishinsky

Illustrated by Dean Griffiths

Scholastic Canada Ltd.

Toronto New York London Auckland Sydney
Mexico City New Delhi Hong Kong Buenos Aires

Dedication
In memory of my mom, a great storyteller

Acknowledgements
Many thanks to the hard-working Maple Tree team—Sheba Meland, Anne
Shone, Grenfell Featherstone, Deborah Bjorgan, Cali Hoffman, Dawn Todd,
and Erin Walker—for their insightful comments and steadfast support.
Special thanks to Dean Griffiths and Claudia Dávila for their engaging
and energetic illustrations and design.

Design & art direction: Claudia Dávila
Illustrations: Dean Griffiths

ISBN-13: 978-0-545-99322-7
ISBN-10: 0-545-99322-9
School Market Edition

Published by arrangement with Maple Tree Press Inc.
This edition published in 2010 by Scholastic Canada Ltd.,
604 King Street West, Toronto, Ontario M5V 1E1, Canada.

6 5 4 3 2 1   Printed in Canada   10 11 12 13 14 15

CONTENTS

HOW IT ALL BEGAN

Emily and Matt couldn't believe their luck. They discovered an old dresser full of strange objects in the tower of Emily's house. They also found a note from Emily's Great-Aunt Miranda: "The sled is yours. Fly it to wonderful adventures."

They found a sled right behind the dresser! When they sat on it, shimmery gold words appeared:

> *Rub the leaf*
> *Three times fast.*
> *Soon you'll fly*
> *To the past.*

The sled rose over Emily's house. It flew over their town of Glenwood. It sailed out of a cloud and into the past. Their adventures on the flying sled had begun! Where will the sled take them next? Turn the page to find out.

Underground
Railroad
October 1858

1

Underground Railroad

"My cousin Maria is so lucky!" said Matt.

Emily looked up from her drawing. She was sketching a picture of the two of them soaring through the air on the Canadian Flyer sled. She uncurled her legs and sat up in the big wicker chair on the back porch.

"Why's Maria lucky?" she asked.

Matt sat down beside her. He pulled a crumpled postcard out of the pocket of his shorts and handed it to Emily.

"Look what she's doing with her family

this summer." He pointed to the picture on the postcard. It showed a train zooming past a sparkling blue river.

"Where's the train going?" asked Emily.

"Right across Canada. I wish I could travel by train. Trains are awesome. They take you to amazing places."

"So do magic sleds," said Emily.

"I know," said Matt. "But wouldn't it be fun if the sled flew us to a train from long ago?"

"I think I saw something in the dresser with a label about a train. Or was it a railroad? I'm not sure."

Matt jumped up. "That's great! What are we waiting for? Let's check it out."

Emily stood up. She popped her sketchbook into the back pocket of her denim shorts. "I can't wait to draw an old train," she said. "Do you have your recorder with you?"

"Of course. I never leave home without it!" Matt patted his pocket.

"Good," said Emily. She opened the back door to her house. Matt followed her up the creaky stairs to the tower room.

Emily hurried over to the mahogany dresser and opened the second drawer. She pointed to a black and white feather. It was labelled *Underground Railroad, October 1858.*

"I don't know what a feather has to do with a railroad," she said. "But a railroad means trains, right?"

"Right. And maybe these trains go underground. Maybe it's a subway."

"Did they have subways in 1858?" asked Emily.

"I don't know. Maybe this was the first one. Wouldn't that be fantastic?"

"But I still don't understand what a feather

has to do with a train," said Emily, examining the black and white feather.

"There's only one way to find out," said Matt. "Let's take the sled up!"

Emily and Matt pulled the sled out from behind the dresser and hopped on.

The magic words instantly appeared.

Rub the leaf
Three times fast.
Soon you'll fly
To the past.

Emily rubbed the maple leaf, and they were enveloped in fog. When it cleared, they were flying above Emily's house, above the trees, and above Glenwood. They soared higher.

"I can't wait to see that underground train!" Matt called as they flew into a fluffy white cloud.

2

Shhh

"We're landing!" called Emily as the sled burst out of the cloud.

"It's so dark, I can't see anything. Where are we?" asked Matt.

"I don't know. But we're going down fast!"

The sled bumped down.

Matt and Emily slid off the sled and onto a dirt floor.

"It smells in here," said Matt.

Emily held her nose and grimaced. "It smells like a chicken coop. I thought we were landing on a train. Not in a stinky—what is this place?"

"I think it's a basement in an old house," said Matt. "Look over there. There's a lantern in the window."

A black lantern with a lit candle was perched on the ledge of a small grimy window.

"And look at our clothes," said Emily.

She had on a long blue and white flowered dress and laced-up black shoes. Matt wore long, black pants, black suspenders, and a white shirt.

"These must be 1858 clothes," said Matt. "My grandfather has a pair of suspenders like these. I put them on once. They're fun." Matt snapped the suspenders.

"Shhh, Matt. I hear something."

They heard *clip-clop* and the crunching of gravel from outside.

"It sounds like a horse," said Matt.

Emily ran to the tiny window and peered out. She couldn't see anything. She looked around the basement. "Where's the door? How do we get out of here?"

Matt shook his head. "I don't know. Let's check the walls. Maybe there's a secret door."

Matt and Emily tapped all the walls, but nothing opened.

"We have to get out of here. It's creepy," groaned Emily.

"What's this?" asked Matt. He touched a rough spot on the wall near the small window.

Emily squinted to see. "Someone carved the word PUSH!" she exclaimed. "Could it mean…?"

"Yes!" Matt pushed against the word. The wall began to move. Emily and Matt pushed more. The wall opened. It was a secret door!

Emily and Matt ran up narrow rickety steps to another door. They slid open a heavy wooden latch and looked out into the moonless night.

"There's a horse and wagon outside," said Emily. "But where's the Underground Railroad?"

"What if the sled sent us to the wrong place?" asked Matt. "What if we're on the wrong adventure?"

"Then how do we get out of here?" asked

Emily. "And who is that man?" Emily pointed to a tall, burly man with red hair and a thick beard. The man jumped off the wagon and strode toward the house.

He smiled when he reached the door. "I am Dr. Ross, a friend with friends," he said in a quiet voice. "You are expecting us."

Emily glanced at Matt. He looked as confused as she was. Who did this Dr. Ross think they were? Who was "us?" Emily couldn't see anyone except Dr. Ross outside or in the wagon. And where was the Underground Railroad?

"I'm Emily Bing, and this is Matt Martinez," she said. "We just got here."

"I see," said Dr. Ross, peering at them. "I can tell you are worried. But do not fear. I have checked. There are no slave catchers anywhere."

"Slave catchers? I don't understand," said Matt. "Where's the Underground Railroad?"

Dr. Ross rubbed his beard. "Hmm," he said. "You children were not told the true meaning of the words. The Underground Railroad is right here where you stand. You are part of it. Now, come meet the passengers."

3

Listen!

The children followed Dr. Ross to the wagon.

"I am pleased to have your help," he said. "I know we have arrived later than agreed, but we waited until dark to avoid detection. Now, let me introduce you."

Dr. Ross lifted a thick bale of hay from the top of the wagon. A tall African American woman, two twin boys of about six, and a girl of about ten crouched under the hay. They brushed the hay out of their hair and clothing, and stumbled out of the wagon.

Emily and Matt stared at the group standing in front of them.

"This is Sarah and her two sons, Elijah and Sam," said Dr. Ross. "They were slaves on a plantation in Mississippi. And this is Lucy. She was a slave on the same plantation. We hope she will soon be reunited with her older brother in Canada."

Sarah held on to her two boys tightly.

Emily's eyes widened. Were these people really slaves? They looked like ordinary people. "I can't imagine someone owning me," Emily blurted out. "Did they treat you horribly?"

Sarah nodded. Tears sprung into her eyes. She brushed them away with her hand. "We were slaves once," she said. "But we are free now. We thank God, and we thank you all for your kindness."

Sarah's two boys smiled shyly.

Emily and Matt smiled back. They didn't know what to say. How could they tell Dr. Ross and his group that they weren't there to help them? How could they say that they thought they were on an adventure to find a real train?

"Let us hurry inside," said Dr. Ross.

Everyone followed Matt and Emily inside, down the stairs, and into the secret basement room.

"Why is this called the Underground Railroad?" asked Emily.

"It is not a real railroad, of course," said Dr. Ross, as they shut the secret door behind them. "It is a network of escape routes and safe houses like this one. Those of us who help bring slaves to freedom are called conductors. And those of us who provide a safe haven, like the owners of this house, are called station masters. We work in secret. It is as if we were underground."

"How far are you going?" asked Matt.

"Across the Niagara River to Canada. It is not far from where we are right now in Lewistown, New York. But you know that already, children, don't you?"

"We don't know exactly where we are now," said Emily. "We're from Canada, but we got lost."

"Then you must come back to Canada with us. Your family will be worried," said Dr. Ross.

"Will we cross the bridge into Canada?" Lucy asked Dr. Ross.

"After we have rested and eaten, we will try to cross the suspension bridge, just north of Niagara Falls," said Dr. Ross. "But we must be watchful and move quietly. We do not want to be discovered by slave catchers."

4

Don't Move

Everyone sat on the dirt floor as Dr. Ross passed out bread, apples, and cider.

"I'm sorry it is not much, but it is all I have left," he said.

"It is good—better than the food on the plantation," said Lucy.

"How did you get them away from the plantation without getting caught?" Emily asked Dr. Ross.

"I travel around the South, birdwatching," he explained. He pulled a black and white feather out of his jacket to show them. It was the feather they'd seen in the dresser!

"This is from one of the birds I observed on my last journey through the South. Birdwatching is my hobby. It is also my excuse to travel and help slaves. That's how I met Lucy and her grandmother," he explained. "They were picking cotton in the fields when I encountered them. Lucy's grandmother was so ill that she could barely stand. She begged me to help Lucy escape to freedom and join her brother in Canada."

"Gram took care of me when they sold Mama down river five years ago," Lucy explained.

"And Sarah's husband was killed when he tried to run away from the plantation," said Dr. Ross.

"After they killed him, they beat me," said Sarah. She lifted the sleeves of her long dress.

Her arms were slashed and red. "I was afraid they would kill me and my boys."

Matt swallowed hard as he looked at Sarah's arms and listened to Lucy and Sarah's story. How could people be so cruel? Lucy was just a kid. And Sarah hadn't hurt anyone. She just wanted her boys to be safe and free.

"We'll help you," said Matt.

Emily nodded. "We really want to help."

Dr. Ross smiled. "Perhaps there is something you can do, children. In the meantime, let us finish eating and begin our journey. It will be a long and dangerous night."

Dr. Ross walked to the window and peered out. "I don't see or hear anyone. We will leave the horse and wagon here and begin our trek to the bridge."

"Who'll take care of the horse?" asked Emily.

"The station master who owns this safe house. He and his family are away visiting relatives in a near-by town. But he helped us with our plans. It is all arranged. Our job now is to cross the bridge to safety. Let us go."

Everyone stood up. Matt picked up the sled's rope and pulled it along the dirt floor.

"Why do you have a sled?" Dr. Ross asked him. "It is not winter yet."

Emily and Matt glanced at each other. How could they explain about the sled?

"My great-aunt gave it to me," said Emily.

"You wish to take it back to Canada with you?" asked Dr. Ross.

"We have to," said Emily.

"But we must move quickly," said Dr. Ross. "How will you manage with the sled?"

"Don't worry. We'll pull it," said Matt.

"Or carry it," said Emily.

"I must tell you that if the sled slows us down or makes our journey difficult, I will have to ask you to abandon it. We cannot let anything endanger lives."

"We'll take care of it," said Emily.

"We have to," added Matt.

5

Closer

The group quietly filed up the stairs. But just as they opened the basement door, they heard barking and voices outside.

"What is it?" shouted a man. His voice was rough and hard.

"They must be here somewhere," said another man. "The dogs will not stop growling and barking."

No one in the house moved. Elijah and Sam held their mother's hand tightly. Their eyes were wide with fear.

The men began to pound on the door. "Open up! We need to speak to you."

Everyone inside stood still as statues.

Matt swallowed the lump in his throat. Emily's nose began to tickle. She felt a sneeze coming. She held her nose to stop it.

"Open up or we'll break this door down!" The men banged harder.

Emily couldn't stop the sneeze. She grabbed a handkerchief from her pocket and sneezed as quietly as she could into it.

"What was that sound?" asked one of the men.

"I didn't hear anything," said the other. "But look, the dogs are running down the hill. They must smell something that way."

"Hurry! Follow them!" said the first man.

The men's feet pounded away from the house.

The dogs howled and barked like wolves in the night.

Everyone in the house waited and listened. Soon the running and barking grew dimmer. Then the noise stopped.

Could the men have changed directions? Could the dogs have led them elsewhere? Was it safe to go out?

Dr. Ross motioned them not to move. Ten minutes passed. Still no noise from outside.

Twenty minutes.

An hour. No one heard voices or barks.

"The men seem to have gone, but they may be lurking in the bushes. We can't stay here any longer. It will soon be daylight," whispered Dr. Ross.

"Matt and I could go outside and check things out," suggested Emily.

"And if there's anyone there," said Matt,

"we can say we were lost after picking up our sled, so we decided to stop here until daylight."

"And if they ask about the horse and wagon," said Emily, "we can tell them that it belongs to the owner of the house. We can say he's visiting a neighbour, but he promised to give us a lift home in the morning."

"Good thinking, children, but I cannot let you risk yourselves for us. Slave catchers are ruthless," whispered Dr. Ross. "They might not believe you."

Matt gulped. The same thought had gone through his mind. But they had to get out of here. They had to help Dr. Ross and his group.

"You'll see. We'll convince them. We'll be OK," he said.

"And if it's safe for you to come outside, we'll knock on the door three times," said Emily.

"Thank you, children," said Dr. Ross. "We have no choice but to try your plan. We will wait for your signal."

Matt's heart beat hard as they walked back up the rickety stairs. He and Emily unlatched the door and peered outside. They couldn't see anyone. They stepped outside.

The air had turned cold, and a brisk wind blew through the trees. The leaves rustled like blinds against a windowpane. But they didn't hear people or dogs.

They walked toward the horse and wagon. Emily patted the horse's soft nose. The horse shook its head and neighed.

Emily and Matt looked around and then walked into the woods. They peered into the dark.

It was quiet. They looked around and waited. Nothing. No dogs or people—just crickets and squirrels, and the whoosh of the wind through the trees.

"Do you think it's safe?" Emily whispered to Matt.

"I think so," said Matt.

"Let's signal Dr. Ross."

Matt nodded. "I hope we're right. I hope it's safe, otherwise..."

Emily took a deep breath. "I know, but we have to take a chance. Go ahead. Knock."

6

The Bridge

Matt knocked three times. The door squeaked open.

"Have you seen anyone?" asked Dr. Ross.

"No," said Matt. "We think it's safe."

"Are the slave catchers only around here?" asked Emily.

"There are slave catchers on both sides of the border, but most are here, in New York. It will be safer in Canada. Let us go."

Quietly the group filed up the stairs and out of the safe house.

Matt carried the sled so it wouldn't make noise on the ground.

They followed Dr. Ross past the horse and wagon and through the forest. They trekked over rocks and fallen trees. They waded into shallow streams.

They walked and walked.

They listened for men and dogs, but the only sounds were leaves crunching and twigs snapping under their feet. It was hard to see where they were going. The stars were their only light, but Dr. Ross knew the way.

Then, in a clearing, they saw the bridge. It hung like a huge metal chain between New York State and Canada. It was long and wide. They could hear the raging Niagara River below them.

"It's such a long bridge," Emily whispered to Matt.

"And it's close to Niagara Falls. Have you ever seen the falls?" Matt asked in a low voice.

"Once," said Emily. "They're big and beautiful. And scary."

"I wouldn't want to fall into the river near the falls," said Matt.

"I wouldn't want to fall into the river anywhere. It's freezing down there." Emily shivered.

Dr. Ross motioned for them to follow him across the bridge. Emily and Lucy walked first. Sarah followed with her two boys. Matt was the last one in line.

"This bridge is mighty high," said Lucy in a low voice. "I am dizzy just looking down."

"Don't think about it and don't look down," said Emily. "Just keep walking."

They walked on a few steps.

Emily turned to glance at Lucy. Her teeth were clenched, and she was taking deep breaths.

"We'll be across soon," Emily whispered, squeezing her hand. "You can make it!"

Lucy squeezed Emily's hand back. She swallowed and nodded.

They walked on farther, and then they heard a dog barking. It seemed to come from across the bridge on the Canadian side. Dr. Ross raised his hand to tell them to stop walking.

They waited. The barking grew louder. They heard men's voices! They could hear men running and dogs howling.

"Turn back!" Dr. Ross whispered urgently. "Run! Hurry! Get off the bridge!"

Everyone raced back toward the American side of the bridge. This time they didn't care that they were up high. All they could think

about was getting off the bridge and away from
the slave catchers.

"Quick! Into the woods!" urged Dr. Ross as
they neared the beginning of the bridge. He led
them quickly down a steep embankment.

"Mama!" wailed Elijah. "They're coming!"

"They're going to catch us!" cried Sam. "They're going to take us back!"

"Hush, children. We'll be fine. Keep moving. Don't stop," said Sarah.

"Keep low," said Dr. Ross. "I know a cave. It's not far away. We can make it, but we must hurry."

7

Moses

"Do you see them?" called one of the slave catchers.

"Without a moon, who can see anything?" said the other man. "The dogs have stopped barking. Maybe we should turn back. Maybe they went another way."

"What other way? The only other way is by boat, but who'd be fool enough to take out a boat on a blustery night like this? And it's going to rain soon. The river is going to be wild tonight."

"Let's wait on the bridge. They may try crossing again."

"Thank goodness," said Dr. Ross as they sped through the woods. "Keep going!"

Even though they could no longer hear the men or their dogs, every sound made them jump. Every movement in the grass made their hearts race. There could be other slave catchers in the woods. Dr. Ross explained that many people wanted to earn the reward for capturing runaway slaves.

"This way," said Dr. Ross, pointing to a cave carved into the rock near the water's edge.

The group scurried into the cave. Emily shivered. It was damp, cold, and dark inside. They crouched down on the dirt floor.

"Mama! There's a bear over there!" cried Elijah. He was shaking and pointing to the far wall of the cave.

Dr. Ross lit a match and held it up. "See, Elijah. It is not a bear but a shadow." He patted Elijah on the back.

"What do we do now, Dr. Ross? I am so tired," said Lucy.

"I know. We are all weary from hiding and running. But a boat will come soon, and we will cross into Canada by the river. The bridge is too dangerous tonight."

"But the river is dangerous, too," said Matt.

"We have no choice," said Dr. Ross. "It is our only way across. And you heard those slave catchers. They do not believe anyone would be foolish enough to cross on such a cold, damp night. But we will. And we will make it!"

"Where's the boat?" asked Emily.

"My friend, Harriet Tubman, is waiting on the other side. We arranged that if we did not make it across the bridge, she would come by boat and take us across."

"Harriet Tubman? The Black Moses?" said Lucy. Her eyes shone.

'Yes. Some call her Moses," said Dr. Ross.

"Moses, like in the Bible?" asked Matt.

"Yes, like in the Bible. But this Moses is a woman," said Dr. Ross.

"We heard tales of Moses," said Sarah. "She leads people to freedom."

"There is no one like her. She is fearless," said Dr. Ross. "Now, let us all rest here for an hour. We will need all our strength to cross safely. We must be alert and ready for anything."

"Sam and Elijah are resting already," said Sarah, smiling.

Emily looked at the two boys. They were curled up asleep beside their mother.

Emily tried to close her eyes. She tossed and turned on the hard ground, but the cave was damp and cold.

She looked over at Matt. He was tossing and turning, too. "I can't rest," she whispered.

"Me neither," said Matt, "but everyone else is, except for Dr. Ross."

Dr. Ross was up and pacing. He kept checking his pocket watch and peering outside.

"I will return in a moment," he told Emily and Matt. "I want to check the river."

Dr. Ross stepped out of the cave.

"Who would have thought we'd be in a cave and about to take a boat ride across a wild river in the middle of the night?" said Emily.

"This underground train adventure is turning out to be even more amazing than a ride on a real train," said Matt.

He pulled out his recorder and walked to the entrance of the cave, so he wouldn't wake anyone.

"This is Matt reporting," he said in a low voice. "We're in a cave in New York State in 1858. Emily and I are about to take a boat across the Niagara River to bring slaves to freedom in Canada."

"Where is Dr. Ross?" asked Emily, walking over to Matt after a while had passed. "He said he'd be gone a minute, but it's more like twenty minutes. Maybe he saw the slave catchers. Maybe they stopped him. And if they did, what will we do?"

8

Wake Up!

"There he is!" called Matt, as Dr. Ross rushed back to the cave.

"Wake up. Moses is here to help us across," said Dr. Ross.

Sam and Elijah rubbed their eyes and yawned.

"Hurry, children," said Sarah.

Lucy opened her eyes. "I know we will make it this time. Moses has come to help!"

The group quickly gathered up their belongings and followed Dr. Ross out of the cave.

It was still dark as they stumbled over the jagged and slippery rocks toward the river.

"I hear thunder," said Emily.

"And I see lightning!" said Matt. "It's going to rain."

"We can't stop now," said Dr. Ross.

"There's the boat," said Emily.

"And there is Moses!" exclaimed Lucy.

A short, black woman stood at the riverbank beside a large raft. The raft had been knocked together from long, mismatched pieces of wood.

"It doesn't look like much," said Harriet Tubman. "But it will take us to the other side. To freedom."

Matt and Emily glanced at the raft and then at each other.

The waves pounded against the raft and the rocky shore.

Could this shaky-looking raft get them across the wild Niagara River?

"Mama, I don't want to go in that boat. I'm scared!" cried Sam, clutching his mother's skirt.

Elijah said nothing. He stared at the raft and snuggled closer to Sarah.

"Miss Tubman has crossed the river on this raft many times. She knows the river well, and so do I," said Dr. Ross.

"But, Mama!" wailed Sam.

"Hush, Sam," said Sarah. "We must listen to these good people. They will bring us to freedom."

One by one, they carefully stepped onto the raft. When Matt and Emily began to lift the sled on board, Harriet Tubman said, "We don't have room for *that*."

"Please," said Emily. "It's not heavy."

"We have to take it back to Canada. It won't be in anyone's way," said Matt. "Please, let us take it."

"If it gets in the way, I will dump it in the river," said Harriet. "I will not lose a passenger for a sled."

Matt gulped. "We'll take care of it," he promised. He glanced at Emily. He knew she was thinking the same thing. They couldn't let the sled go overboard, no matter what.

Matt and Emily lifted the sled aboard as they climbed onto the raft. Harriet handed everyone a cotton blanket.

"Keep seated," she ordered them. "Dr. Ross and I will row, and you must all remain calm. Do not get up no matter what happens, or the boat will tip. I have never lost a passenger, and I don't aim to now!"

Then, with one hard shove of an oar, Harriet

Tubman pushed the raft away from shore.

They swirled into the Niagara River. The raft immediately began to spin like a top, but Harriet and Dr. Ross held the oars tightly. They kept the raft steady. But they couldn't stop the icy river water from drenching the passengers as the raft twisted and turned.

"Cover yourselves with the blankets," said Harriet. The passengers wrapped themselves in the blankets, but the water still seeped through the cotton and through their clothes.

"I'm so wet and cold," groaned Emily. "I feel like a fish."

"Me too," said Matt, shivering. "And it's going to rain in a minute. Look!" He pointed up at the sky. It was dotted with dark, menacing clouds. "We're going to get even wetter."

"I fear you are right," said Dr. Ross.

No sooner had Dr. Ross said those words

than a streak of lightning bolted across the sky. The rain began to pour down in sheets.

The waves on the river rose higher. The raft dipped up and down like a bronco in a rodeo. It felt as if it would spill them all into the raging water.

The passengers huddled together under their wet blankets as Dr. Ross and Harriet steered the raft. Water dripped down their faces and soaked into their clothes, too. But they never stopped. They kept the raft moving.

"What if we tip into the river?" Emily whispered to Matt. "What if—"

But Matt couldn't hear her words. The wind and a loud clap of thunder drowned them out.

9

Sit Down!

"What did you say?" Matt shouted to Emily.

"I said what if we drown?" Emily called back.

"We won't," said Matt.

"The rain is slowing down," said Sarah.

"Halleluiah!" shouted Lucy. "It is!"

"We will soon be across," said Harriet. She pressed her hands into the oars and rowed harder.

"Thank goodness," said Dr. Ross. "I am weary, as I am sure you all are."

"The shore is close, but the sun is rising," said Harriet. "We must row even harder and faster. We have to reach land before the sun comes up. Darkness is our friend. Light is not. The slave catchers can see us in the light."

"If there are slave catchers in Canada, why is it safer there?" asked Matt.

"The government of Canada does not allow slavery. The slave catchers try to snatch slaves back with any means they have, even in Canada. Sometimes they succeed," said Harriet. "But we will not let them."

"We will never go back," said Lucy. "No matter what." Her face looked determined.

Sarah patted Lucy's arm. "None of us will go back to that miserable life," said Sarah. "Can you see Canada? I cannot."

"Look over there!" Emily pointed. "See that dark, flat line? It's the shore. It's Canada!"

"Yes. I see it now. Canada." Sarah mouthed the word as if it were a prayer.

Lucy's eyes shone like lanterns. "I wish Gram was here. I wish she knew that we are about to be free."

"Mama!" said Sam. "I am so tired. I want to get off this raft now. How soon will we be in Canada?"

"Soon, my child," said Sarah. "Look there. Do you see it?"

"No," said Sam. "Where is it?"

And before they could stop him, Sam slid over toward Emily. He stood up to look.

"Sam!" screamed Sarah. "Sit down!"

"Sit down *now*," Harriet ordered him. "You will tip this raft."

Sam tried to sit back down, but he caught his foot on the edge of a board. He fell forward and slid to the raft's edge!

Sam's hands plunged into the icy water.
"Please! Help!" he screamed.

Matt leaned over and grabbed him by his
pant leg, but Sam's pants ripped.

Sam slid farther. Matt grabbed him by his middle. Emily leaned over to help.

Together they yanked at the sobbing little boy. With one hard tug, they pulled Sam back aboard the raft.

Sarah wrapped her arms around her son.

She held him close and rocked him in her arms. Tears streamed down her face. "Thank you," she said to Matt and Emily. "If it weren't for you, I would have lost him."

10

A Sketch in Time

The raft swung close to shore. Now they could clearly see rocks, bushes, and trees.

Swiftly, Harriet and Dr. Ross steered toward land.

"We must get everyone off the raft quickly. The sun is almost up, and the slave catchers will be out hunting again," said Dr. Ross.

"As soon as we are on land, follow me. There is a safe house nearby," said Harriet.

"You will be given dry clothes, and you can rest there," explained Dr. Ross.

The raft tapped against the shore. Harriet climbed out and tied the raft to a boulder. One by one, the wet and weary passengers stepped onto the rocky beach.

"Today you start your first day as free people. We must make sure those slave catchers never change that!" Harriet told them.

As she stumbled out of the raft, Emily's sketchbook fell out of her pocket.

"Hey, Em," said Matt. "Your sketchbook fell!"

"Thanks," said Emily picking it up. The first page was wet, but the rest of it was still dry. Emily popped it back into the pocket of her dress.

The group began to walk up a hill when Harriet signalled them to stop. "I hear something," she whispered.

Everyone stopped moving and waited.

Soon they could all hear the loud voices of men and dogs. The slave catchers were coming.

They were just up the hill! They had to do something fast.

Emily quickly motioned Matt to follow her. Matt nodded and signalled to Dr. Ross and Harriet.

Emily and Matt hurried up the hill. Two large men and their two snarling dogs greeted them.

"You two see a group of slaves down by the river?" grunted the taller of the men.

"There's no one down by the river," said Emily.

"We heard a group of slaves might be crossing," said the other man.

"Who'd cross in that storm?" said Matt.

The first man's eyes narrowed as he stared at them. "So what were you two doing down by the river? And what do you need a sled for in October?" he asked.

"The sled belongs to Emily's great-aunt," said Matt. "And we're taking it home."

"And we were looking for my sketchbook," said Emily. "I dropped it by the river, and I was afraid it would be ruined in the rain. I drew some really good pictures."

Emily pulled the sketchbook out of her pocket and showed the men. "See there's one of a ship and another of—"

"I have no time for silly pictures," barked the second man, waving Emily away. "We're after slaves, but I see they are not here." He turned to his friend. "I told you that no one would be crazy enough to row across the Niagara in that storm."

With that, the slave catchers and their dogs headed away from the hill.

"Phew!" said Emily, leaning against a tree.

"Let's tell everyone that the slave catchers are gone," said Matt. "I hope they're all still down the hill."

11

Safe and Free

Emily and Matt raced down the hill. They spied the group behind a clump of trees at the water's edge.

"The slave catchers left," said Emily.

"They didn't think we could get across the river," said Matt. "But we did!"

Dr. Ross beamed. "Thank you, children. You have helped us in many ways. We are grateful that you joined us on this journey."

"We are too," said Matt.

"Now let us hurry to the next safe house,"

said Harriet. "Soon you will get help to start a new, free life in Canada. "

They all followed Harriet farther along the river's edge.

"Let me carry the sled this time," Emily told Matt.

Emily picked the sled up. Some wet leaves had fallen on it. She brushed them off. As she did, she saw words forming on the front of the sled.

Emily tapped Matt on the shoulder. "Matt, look!" she whispered.

Matt looked down at the front of the sled. He saw the shimmery gold words.

> *You've helped your friends.*
> *They're safe and free.*
> *Now rub the leaf.*
> *Quick—One! Two! Three!*

"We have to tell the group to go on without us," said Matt.

"I know. The sled is telling us to go home."

Matt rushed ahead to Harriet and Dr. Ross. "We know where we are now, and we're not far from home. We have to go."

"Then we will bid you farewell. I hope we meet again," said Dr. Ross. He shook Matt's hand.

Emily put the sled down. She and Matt shook hands with every person in the group. They hugged Lucy, Sarah, and the boys.

"Hurry!" said Harriet. "We cannot stay here a moment longer. We wish you a safe journey, children."

With a quick wave to Emily and Matt, Harriet Tubman and Dr. Ross led the group away.

When they were out of sight, Emily and

Matt hopped on the sled. Emily rubbed the leaf. Soon they were flying above the trees, above the river, above Niagara Falls, and into the fluffy white cloud.

The sled landed with a soft thump in the tower room.

"It was so dark and wet on that adventure that I had no chance to draw even one picture," said Emily as she slipped off the sled. "I don't want to forget what everyone looked like."

"Why don't you draw now?" suggested Matt.

"I will." She plunked down on the floor of the attic and began to sketch.

Matt sat beside her and peered over her shoulder. "What are you drawing?" he asked.

"Lucy, Sarah, and the boys living in Canada as free people. I hope they have a good, happy life. And I hope Lucy meets her brother again."

"Me too," said Matt. "And I hope the sled will take us on a real train adventure one day soon!"

Emily patted the sled like an old friend. "You never know. It just might!"

MORE ABOUT...

After their adventure, Emily and Matt wanted to know more about the Underground Railroad. Turn the page for their favourite facts.

Emily's Top Ten Facts

1. There aren't many records about how many slaves used the Underground Railroad because it was so secret. Some people think that as many as 40,000 slaves used it to escape to freedom.

2. Many slaves escaped to Canada through New York, Michigan, and Ohio.

3. In the early 1800s, American law said that black people were household property. This means the law did not consider slaves as human beings.

4. From 1827, New York State did not allow anyone to own a slave.

5. In 1791, Lt. Governor John Graves Simcoe did not allow slaves to be brought to Upper Canada for sale. Slavery was totally abolished in Canada in 1833.

6. The Niagara Suspension Bridge was built in 1851.

7. In 1864, after a heavy freeze, the suspension bridge wires were unfastened so they wouldn't tear. Before they could be re-attached, the centre of the bridge collapsed in a terrible storm. That was the end of the Niagara Suspension Bridge.

> Yikes! We could have been on the bridge then! —M.

8. Many people in Lewiston, New York, helped slaves escape to freedom.

9. Josiah Tryon, a Lewiston tailor, made slave catchers colourful jackets as gifts. This clever trick told people in Lewistown who the slave hunters were.

10. In 1853, Ben Hockley, a slave from Tennessee, escaped to Lewiston, New York. He used a gate as a raft to cross the Niagara River. He was almost swept away, but a steamer boat rescued him.

> Imagine if he went over Niagara Falls! —M.

67

Matt's Top Ten Facts

1. The "trains" on the Underground Railroad were really large farm wagons that hid slaves and the "tracks" were backcountry roads.

> We saw those "trains" and walked down those "tracks."
> -E.

2. Harriet Beecher Stowe wrote a book, *Uncle Tom's Cabin*, about the terrible way slaves were treated. It was based on the life of a slave called Josiah Henson.

3. After Josiah Henson escaped to freedom, he settled in Ontario, and helped other slaves escape.

4. When President Abraham Lincoln met Harriet Beecher Stowe he said, "So you're the little lady who started the Big War." The war he was talking about was the American Civil War. When it was over in 1865, all the slaves in the United States were declared free.

5. People like Harriet Beecher Stowe were called "abolitionists." Abolitionists wanted to stop slavery forever.

6. Many "conductors" and slaves used the North Star to help guide them to freedom.

7. On their way to freedom in Canada, some slaves were hidden in trunks, barrels, and even in coffins.

I hope they had good air holes! -E.

8. Sometimes slaves wore disguises when they escaped.

9. Some people helping slaves escape used secret codes to pass messages that slaves were on their way to freedom.

10. Levi and Catherine Coffin were Quaker abolitionists in the United States who hid many slaves in their house. They helped over 2,000 slaves escape to freedom.

So You Want to Know...
FROM AUTHOR FRIEDA WISHINSKY

When I was researching this book, my friends wanted to know more about the Underground Railroad. I told them that my story is based on historical fact and that some of the characters like Dr. Alexander Ross and Harriet Tubman were real people. I made up other characters like Lucy, Sarah, and her two boys. I also answered these questions:

How did people become slaves?

Plantation owners needed people to work on their cotton, sugar, or tobacco fields. Slaves were free people captured in Africa and brought to America in ships. The journey was horrible, and many people died of hunger and disease even before they reached America. Once in America, they were sold at auctions like cattle.

The children of slaves from Africa were often separated from their families. Sometimes a mother, father, brother, or sister was sold to another plantation owner and never saw their family again.

How did Alexander Ross become a conductor on the Underground Railroad?

Alexander Ross grew up in Canada in a family opposed to slavery. Alexander decided that when he grew up he too would help slaves escape to freedom. When he was twenty-three, that's just what he began to do. He used his interest in birds as an excuse to travel to the southern United States. Of course, he didn't just check out birds but helped slaves escape to freedom. He led many to freedom himself.

Was Harriet Tubman ever a slave herself?

Harriet Tubman was born a slave in Maryland around the year 1820. She and her family of ten brothers and sisters worked hard but were still whipped by their owners. When Harriet heard that her family was going to be separated, she decided to run away to freedom. She escaped slavery in 1849.

How did she escape?

Her father was a woodsman. Harriet used the knowledge he gave her of the woods, the stars, and wilderness survival to run away. She also knew how to hide without being heard or seen. She fled safely to Philadelphia, Pennsylvania.

How did she help others to freedom?

Harriet used many different means to help slaves escape. She wore disguises. She used codes and signals. She was smart, determined, and never hesitated or showed fear.

What did Alexander Ross do once the Civil War ended and the slaves in the United States were freed?

Dr. Ross was awarded many honours. He was knighted by the Emperor of Russia and given medals by the leaders of Greece, Portugal, and other countries. He continued his practice as a doctor, although later he became the Ontario Treasurer, Commissioner of Agriculture, and a Consul in Belgium and Denmark.

What did Harriet Tubman do during and after the Civil War?

Harriet returned to the United States during the Civil War. She worked as a nurse and an army scout. After the war, she helped women fight for equal rights. She lived in Auburn, New York, where she aided poor and elderly African Americans. She died in 1913, when she was around 93.

About the Author

Frieda Wishinsky, a former teacher, is an award-winning picture- and chapter-book author, who has written many beloved and bestselling books for children. Frieda enjoys using humour and history in her work, while exploring new ways to tell a story. Her books have earned much critical praise, including a nomination for a Governor General's Award in 1999. In addition to the books in the *Canadian Flyer Adventures* series, Frieda has published *What's the Matter with Albert?*, *A Quest in Time*, and *Manya's Dream* with Maple Tree Press. Frieda lives in Toronto.

About the Illustrator

Gordon Dean Griffiths realized his love for drawing very early in life. At the age of 12, halfway through a comic book, Dean decided that he wanted to become a comic book artist and spent every spare minute of the next few years perfecting his art. In 1995 Dean illustrated his first children's book, *The Patchwork House*, written by Sally Fitz-Gibbon. Since then he has happily illustrated over a dozen other books for young people and is currently working on several more, including the *Canadian Flyer Adventures* series. Dean lives in Duncan, B.C.

Send In Your
Top Ten Facts

If you enjoyed this adventure as much as Matt and Emily did, maybe you'd like to collect your own facts about the Underground Railroad, too.

To find out how to send in your favourite facts, visit **www.mapletreepress.com/canadianflyeradventures**. Maple Tree Press will choose the very best facts that are sent in to make *Canadian Flyer Adventures* Readers' Top Ten Lists.

Each reader who sends in a fact that is selected for a Top Ten List will receive a new book in the *Canadian Flyer Adventures* series! (If more than one person sends in the same fact and it is chosen, the first person to submit that fact will be the winner.)

We look forward to hearing from you!